ABIYOYO

ABIYOYO

Based on a South African Lullaby and Folk Story

text by Pete Seeger
illustrations by Michael Hays

Macmillan Publishing Company
New York

Collier Macmillan Publishers
London

Dedicated with love to
Dan and Cassie,
Mika and Tao,
Tinya and Kitama
– P. S.

For Polly
– M.H.

Macmillan Publishing Company
866 Third Avenue, New York, N.Y. 10022
Collier Macmillan Canada, Inc.

Printed in the United States of America

10 9 8 7 6 5 4 3 2 1

The text of this book is set in 14 pt. Plantin.
The illustrations are in oil on linen.

Library of Congress Cataloging-in-Publication Data

Seeger, Pete, date.
Abiyoyo.
Summary: Banished from the town for making mischief,
a little boy and his father are welcomed back when they
find a way to make the dreaded giant Abiyoyo disappear.
[1. Magicians – Fiction. 2. Giants – Fiction]
I. Hays, Michael, date, ill. II. Title.
PZ7.S4517Ac 1986 [E] 85-15341
ISBN 0-02-781490-4

I adapted this story from an old South African folktale. Once, putting my children to sleep, I tried to sing them a lullaby I'd just learned out of a book. But, when children get to be three or four years old, they realize that lullabyes are propaganda songs. "No! No! We want a story."

At the foot of the page, the book said, "This lullaby is part of an ancient tale about a monster who eats people. The parents get it dancing, and when it falls down in a fit, it is dispatched by the parents." I built the whole story on that footnote.

My children asked that the story be repeated the next night and the next. After a few months, I tried performing it onstage and have done it ever since, acting out the parts, dancing around the stage like a fool.

Now, with Michael Hays retelling the story of Abiyoyo with his pictures, others may tell it in their own way, perhaps act it out, or even change it.

Change it? Yes.

It's important to say no to technology at times. Books are a great invention, but we should remember that it is fun to reinvent stories, to tell stories in the dark to children.

When we do this, we have the opportunity to change the words, to adapt them to some specific occasion. Thus, to children and now grandchildren, I have found myself retelling stories that I have read or heard, boiling down long plays or books to twenty or thirty minutes. Or sometimes I'll expand a shorthand account from the Jewish Christian Bible and flesh it out with descriptions and characters and dialogue. Gradually I have learned to build suspense, use pauses and repetition and rhythm, and avoid unnecessary adjectives.

Don't say "I'm no good as a storyteller." Shakespeare and Tolstoy couldn't tell a story either when they were only six months old. Practice may not make perfect, but it sure as hell makes for improvement. Who wants to be perfect anyway? Remember Ambrose Bierce's definition: "A-chieve-ment: The end of endeavor; the beginning of disgust." I know Michael Hays agrees that children who like to draw can have fun drawing their own versions of Abiyoyo faced by the small boy with the ukelele.

The story has grown on me since I put it together during the Frightened Fifties. These were the years when Senator McCarthy was riding high and the House Un-American Activities Committee was getting people fired for their beliefs. Only years later did I realize the various meanings that could be attached to the story. I still feel that music, dance, and all arts are important tools to help the human race survive, subduing the beast in all of us.

But what is the "right" way to tell the story? Time will tell. If enough parents tell the right stories, perhaps a planet may yet be living one hundred years from now, with parents on it, retelling stories to children.

– Pete Seeger

Once upon a time, there was a little boy who played the ukelele. Around town he'd go, *Clink, clunk, clonk, clink, clunk!* The grown-ups would say, "Take that thing out of here!"

Not only that. The boy's father got in trouble. The boy's father was a magician. He had a magic wand. He'd go *Zoop!* *Zoop!* and make things disappear.

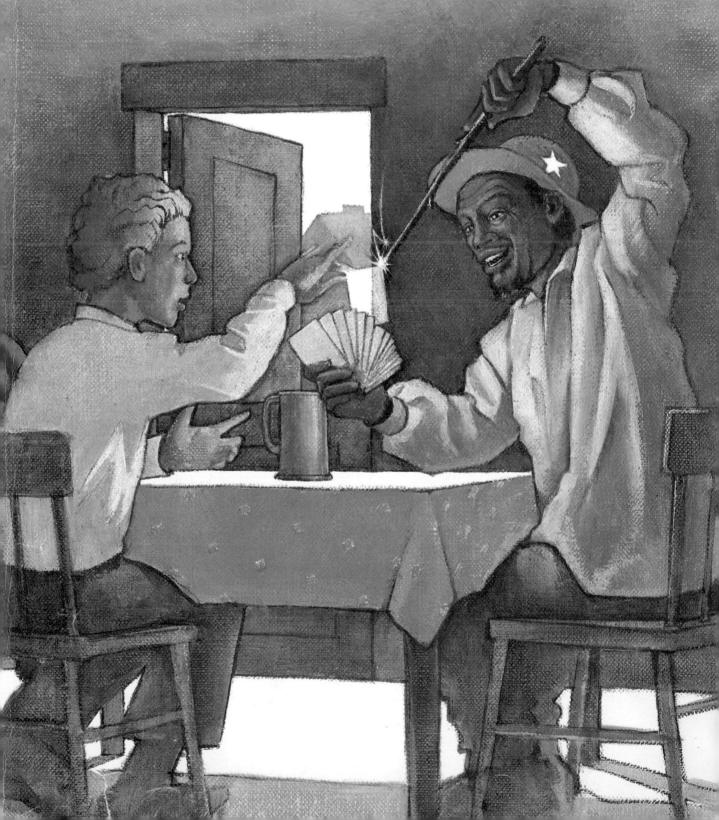

But he played too many tricks on people.

He'd come up to someone about to drink a nice cold glass of something. *Zoop!* The glass disappears.

Someone doing a hard job of work, *ztt, ztt, ztt*. Up comes the father with his magic wand. *Zoop!* No saw.

He'd come up to someone about to sit down after a hard day's work. *Zoop!* No chair.

People said to the father, "You get out of here, too. Take
your magic wand and your tricks, and you and your son just git!"

The boy and his father were ostracized. That means, they made 'em live on the edge of town.

Now in this town they used to tell stories. The old people used to tell stories about the giants that lived in the old days.

They used to tell about a giant called Abiyoyo. They said he was as tall as a tree and could eat people up. Of course, nobody believed the story, but they told it anyway.

One day, one day, the sun rose blood red over the hill. The
first people got up and looked out the window. They saw a
great big shadow in front of the sun. They could feel the whole
ground shake.

Women screamed. Strong men fainted.
"Run for your lives! Abiyoyo's coming!"

He comes to the sheep pasture. He grabs a whole sheep. *Yeowp!* He comes to the cow pasture. He grabs a whole cow. *Yunk!*

Men yelled, "Grab your most precious possessions and run! Run!"

Just then, the boy and his father woke up.

"Hey, Paw, what's coming over the fields?"

"Why, son, that's Abiyoyo. Oh, if only I could get him to lie down, I could make him disappear."

The boy says, "Come with me, Paw." He grabbed his father by one hand. The father gets the magic wand, and the boy gets his ukelele. They run across the fields.

People yelled, "Don't go near him! He'll eat you alive!"

There was Abiyoyo!

He had long fingernails 'cause he never cut 'em. He had slobbery teeth 'cause he didn't brush 'em, stinking feet 'cause he didn't wash 'em, matted hair 'cause he didn't comb it.

He raised up with his claws. . . .

Just then, the boy whips out his ukelele.

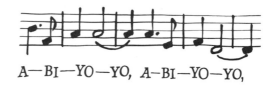

A—BI—YO—YO, A—BI—YO—YO,

Well, you know, the giant had never heard a song about himself before. A foolish grin spread over his face.

And the giant started to dance.

A–BI–YO—YO,   A–BI–YO—YO,

A BI YOYO
A BI YO YO

The boy went faster.

A–BI–YO-YO, BI—YO-YO, YO—YO—YO, A–BI—YO-YO, BI—YO-YO, YO-YO—YO.

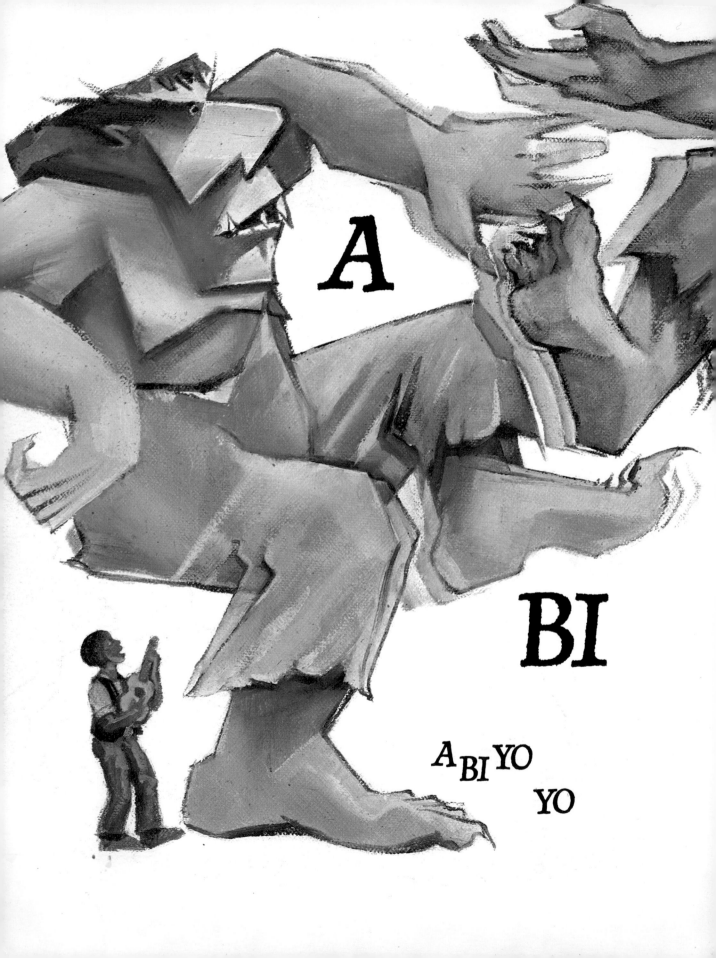

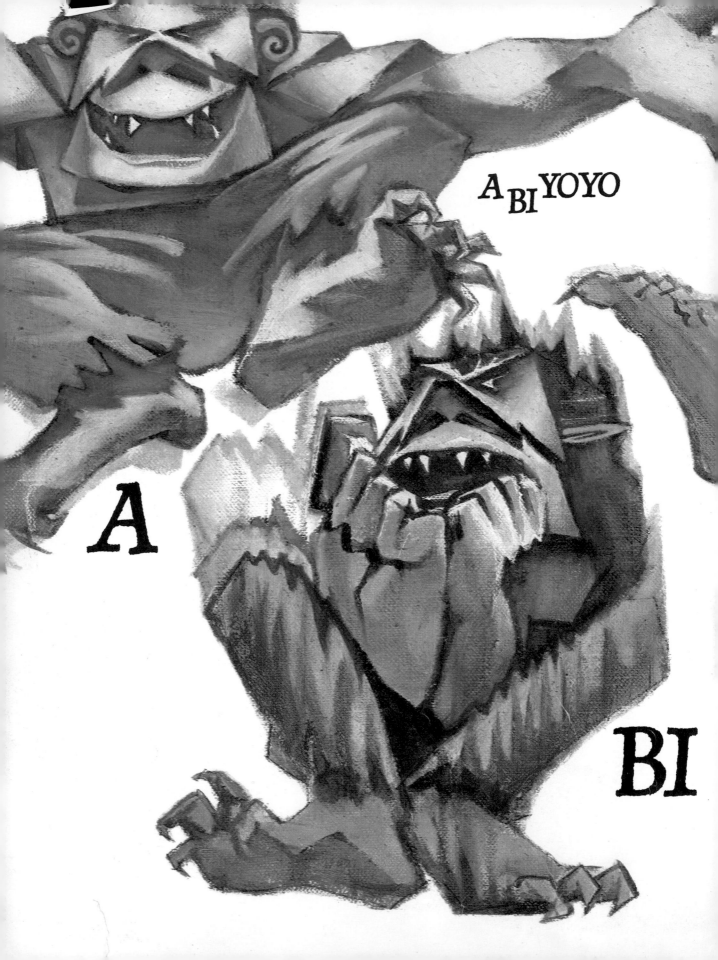

A BI YOYO

A

BI

The giant got out of breath. He staggered. He fell down flat on the ground.

Up steps the father. *Zoop!*

Zoop!

People looked out their windows.
"He's gone! Abiyoyo's disappeared!"

The people ran across the fields.
They lifted the boy and his father up on their shoulders.
They say, "Come back to town. Bring your darn ukelele.
We don't care anymore."

And they all sang.   A–BI–YO—YO,   A–BI–YO—YO,

A—BI—YO—YO,   A—BI—YO—YO,   A—BI—YO—YO, BI—YO—YO, YO—YO—YO,

A—BI—YO—YO,   A—BI—YO—YO,   A—BI—YO—YO,   A—BI—YO—YO,   A—BI—

YO-YO, BI—YO-YO, YO—YO—YO,   A—BI—YO—YO, BI—YO-YO, YO—YO—YO.